THE MYSTERY OF Mimi's Haunted Book Shop

Editor: Janice Baker
Cover Illustration: Dana Cohen
Content Design: Randolyn Friedlander

Gallopade International is introducing SAT words that kids need to know in each
new book that we publish. The SAT words are bold in the story. Look for each
word in the special SAT glossary. Happy Learning!!

Gallopade is proud to be a member and supporter of these educational organizations
and associations:

American Booksellers Association
American Library Association
International Reading Association
National Association for Gifted Children
The National School Supply and Equipment Association
The National Council for the Social Studies
Museum Store Association
Association of Partners for Public Lands
Association of Booksellers for Children
Association for the Study of African American Life and History
National Alliance of Black School Educators

Once upon a time...

Hmm, kids keep asking me to write a mystery book. What shall I do?

Mimi

Write one about spiders!

On the *Mystery Girl* airplane ...

I can fly us anywhere!

Or aboard the *Mimi!*

Take me to the Forbidden City!

Or by surfboard, rickshaw, motorbike, camel ...

All great ideas! I can put a lot of history, MYSTERY, legend, lore, and laughs in the books! We can use other boys and girls in the books. It will be educational and fun!

Good stuff!

And so, Mimi, Papa, Christina, and Grant took off aboard the *Mystery Girl* and America's National Mystery Book Series—where the adventure is real and so are the characters! —was born.

START YOUR ADVENTURE TODAY!

READ THE BOOK!

GO ONLINE!

TRACK YOUR ADVENTURES!

APPLY TO BE A CHARACTER!

1
THE IDEA

"I'm so bored!" Mimi complained. She was sitting by the lovely pool in her backyard. It was the middle of summer and she had written all her new books for the last half of the year. Vacation was over, and it was *hot hot hot!*

"Now, Mimi," Christina warned her grandmother. "You know you told me never to say I was bored."

Christina lounged by the pool, and although she didn't want to admit it, she was bored too. School and seeing her friends was still such a long way off. She had already done everything she wanted to this summer, and all her friends seemed to be out of town. She and Grant had been to some cool summer camps, but that was all over, as well.

Mimi sighed. "Yes, I have sure learned my lesson in the past," she said **candidly**. "Every time I say I am bored, something awful happens that gives me more excitement and adventure than I really want!"

"Like what?" asked Grant, yawning. He lolled in the rope hammock hung between two towering oak trees dripping with Spanish moss.

"Like Papa having to be rushed to the Emergency Room in an ambulance, that's what!" said Mimi. She sipped her iced tea garnished with lemon and fresh mint and mumbled to herself.

"What did you say?" Christina asked gently. It was unusual to see Mimi so listless, her laptop computer all closed up, no big, fat book with a bookmark in it, no notepad and pen handy by her side.

"I was just promising myself never to say the B-word again," Mimi confessed. "Never!"

Grant rolled out of the hammock onto the green grass and sprawled face-down like the kind of body detectives draw chalk marks around at a crime scene to show where it fell. He moaned.

"Are you ok, Grant?" Mimi asked, worried. "It's very hot, almost 100 degrees. Are you sick?"

"He might be dehydrated," suggested Christina with a grin. "Maybe I should squirt him with the hose or drag him into the pool to cool him off?"

Grant jumped up, threw his hands on his hips, and growled at his sister: "I am NOT dehydrated."

"Well, what are you then?" Christina asked.

For a moment Grant paused. His boogie board swimsuit sagged below his bellybutton as he exhaled in discouragement and he snatched it back up. He looked warily at his grandmother. "I can't say," he said.

Now Mimi really was worried. "What, Grant? What?! You have to tell me. Please. Now."

Grant shrugged. "What's wrong with me is...is...is...I'M BORED, TOO!"

To Grant's surprise, his grandmother and sister laughed.

"Well, that mystery cat is out of the bag," said Mimi. "I guess it's no secret and no sense not admitting it: We are three bored cookies!"

Christina and Grant were relieved. Their grandmother, Mimi, who wrote kid's mystery books, and their grandfather, Papa, often took them on great mystery adventures aboard the *Mystery Girl* airplane. They hated to complain when they finally had some time to relax, but chilling out seemed to be getting on everyone's nerves—big time!

"What can we do?" Christina asked, knowing Mimi usually had an answer for everything.

"We could go to the movies!" said Grant.

"We've *been* to the movies," Christina moaned. Mimi groaned and nodded her head in agreement.

"We could go play miniature golf!" Grant suggested hopefully. He swatted an invisible golf club across the grass.

"Too hot!" said Mimi.

"More boring than being bored," Christina said.

"Well, then we could...we could...we could...aw, I'm out of ideas," said Grant. He wilted down onto the grass in a sweaty heap.

For a moment, as the nearby fountain gurgled and a hummingbird buzzed at the feeder, they all were silent.

Christina was the first to spy her grandmother's smile. "Tell us, Mimi, what are you thinking?"

Mimi continued to smile her secret smile beneath her big black sun hat. Her green eyes twinkled.

"Come, on, Mimi," Grant urged. "Tell us. You have an idea, don't you? You do! Tell us!"

Their grandmother stuck up a curled forefinger with candy-apple-red polish on the nail and beckoned them closer. The kids gathered around and hovered over the table, where Mimi's computer perched amidst paper plates and cups left from their picnic lunch.

"Yes," Mimi whispered. "I do have an idea. I do!"

2
OH WOE IS PAPA!

As her grandkids waited impatiently, Mimi tucked her laced fingers beneath her chin and said conspiratorily: "I think I should open a book shop!"

"Wow!" said Christina. "That's a great idea! Right here in Peachtree City?"

"Right here, yes!" said Mimi, clapping her hands. "It will be great fun to design it and stock it with all my mystery books and more! I just must call my favorite book store person, Karen Duncan at Omega Books, and get some good advice from her."

"Sounds like work to me," Grant grumbled. "I guess you want me to sweep and paint some old beat-up place?"

Mimi looked surprised. "No, Grant! I'd want you to design the shop's website.

Isn't that what you learned at computer camp this summer?"

"Sure!" said Grant, excited now. "I can do that! It will be fun!"

"What can I do?" Christina asked eagerly. She'd gone to computer camp too and felt a little disappointed that her grandmother had asked Grant to do the website.

"You can help me design the store!" said Mimi. "Paint colors and furnishings. The logo and the signage. I was hoping we might have a tea room, too."

"That's great, Mimi!" Christina said. "I'd love to do all that!" In her mind, Christina imagined a lovely, cute, adorable, modern, clean, bright book shop with a cool café where she and her friends could go after school. "Can we get cousins Avery and Ella and Evan to help us?"

"Great idea!" said Mimi. "Avery can help you with the design. Ella will love to help with the tea room. And Evan..."

Grant finished his grandmother's sentence: "...can make a MESS!"

They all laughed. Evan WAS a mess and making a mess is what he was good at. He was only three and into everything.

"Mimi, why were you whispering earlier?" asked Grant. "Is this idea a secret?"

Mimi peeked at the back door to the house. "Not really," she said. "I just don't think Papa will be too crazy about the idea. You know how he likes to just sort of laze around in the summer. I'm afraid he will think I'll put him to work, or that it will cost too much money."

"Will it?" asked Christina.

Mimi hesitated. "It will! But doesn't it sound like fun?"

"YES!" Christina and Grant cried together. But while Christina had envisioned a cute, contemporary shop, Grant was imagining a "wild west" kind of saloon book shop. He knew Papa would like that, and so would Grant's buddies.

"Hand me my iPhone!" said Mimi. "I'm going to call my real estate friend right now. We'll see when she can show us a great building for our shop!"

Suddenly the back door of the house swung open and Papa, in his swimsuit, bounded out. "What shop?" he asked.

"Uh, oh," said Christina.

"Uh, oh," said Grant.

Papa slumped down into the nearest lawn chair. "Uh, oh?" Papa said. "What's the mysterious Mimi cooked up now to get us in trouble, kids?"

When Mimi nodded, both kids chattered at the same spitfire rate to tell Papa all the details they knew so far about Mimi's new book shop.

Papa didn't smile and he didn't frown. He just listened. Finally he sighed. "Well, all I know is that if Mimi is determined to do this, I might as well get on board. Of course, knowing Mimi, the dadgum shop will turn out to be haunted or something!"

"That would be awful!" said Christina, thinking of her friends not wanting to visit a creepy book store.

"That would be SUPER COOL!" said Grant, thinking how much his friends would love to visit a spooky shop.

They all jumped when the phone rang. Mimi smiled. "That will be the real estate agent calling me back," she said, and swiped the screen to answer the call that would set her **grandiose** idea in motion.

3
THE SEARCH

Mimi was excited. "She says she can show us something very special and unique right now! She's on her way to pick us up! Who wants to go?"

"Me!" shouted Christina, dashing off to get into some dry clothes.

"Me, too!" shouted Grant. He slipped on his flip-flops and was ready to go.

"Tee shirt, too," said Papa.

"Are you coming with us?" Mimi asked hopefully.

Papa grinned. "No way! You think I'd pass up a nice, clean pool empty of screamin' varmints? I'm staying here and enjoying myself. I'm sure I'll see you at the closing...with my checkbook."

The horn of a six-passenger golf cart tooted and they all turned to see Miss Emma, the local real estate agent, eager to jostle them around Peachtree City's 100 miles of golf cart paths. Truly, the paths were far more used by kids to get to school, moms to get to the grocery store, and dads to fetch and carry kids to ballet lessons, swim meets, and the movies.

Soon, they were headed down a shaded path, tooting at other carts and waving at people they knew. Miss Emma seemed to know everyone.

"Where are we going?" Mimi asked her. "You didn't say, but I love surprises. I am sure I will need to look at many, many sites before I choose one."

"No you won't," Miss Emma insisted, with a wave of her diamond-loaded hand. "This place is perfect, absolutely perfect."

"But I thought looking would be part of the fun," Christina said.

Mimi gave her a wink. "It will," she whispered, knowing Christina would be disappointed if they didn't see every available property in town.

"Well, I hope it has a stable, or something," Grant muttered from the back seat. He was thinking he and Papa would like a book shop with a barn and a horse.

"What?" Christina asked.

"Don't worry about it," her brother said. He knew when to keep his mouth shut.

Before long, they were in an older part of town that Mimi was not familiar with. The farmland was hilly and forested. Snaky kudzu vines climbed over everything, creating giant monster shapes. Homes and shops seemed to be few and far between.

"This seems a bit off the beaten path," Mimi noted.

She was ready to insist that Miss Emma turn around. She couldn't imagine having a successful shop in such a remote location.

But suddenly, Miss Emma rounded a corner and came up over a hill. At a crossroads sat an enormous Victorian home, rambling over a huge lot. The home was set back from the street and had gigantic magnolia trees in full bloom all around it.

A round, cone-shaped turret topped by a quirky weathervane added a certain charm. However, this house was one "painted lady" that had been stripped of any color except weather-beaten gray.

At first glance, it seemed ideal. Then, quickly, Mimi realized where they were.

"Why, this isn't a retail shop!" she said. "This isn't even a home. This is..." For a rare moment, Mimi was speechless.

Christina was speechless.

Grant was reading a worn sign at the corner of the lot:

"MANSE FUNERAL HOME."

Miss Emma laughed. "See! I told you it was perfect!"

"FOR WHAT?" Mimi and the kids said together.

"For your new book shop, of course," Miss Emma said with a pout. "Don't you think so?"

Without another word, Mimi bolted from the golf cart. She sashayed up the cobblestone path to the large veranda that encircled the front of the house.

"See that fancy woodwork all across the top of the porch?" she said to Christina, who nodded, but wondered why Mimi was even bothering to look at this beat-up old place. "That's called gingerbread."

Grant came closer and peered up at the once white, now gray and decaying, pieces of fancy wood. "It's cobwebs," he said.

"No, it isn't!" Mimi insisted, pulling out her sparkly red reading glasses. She, too, peered at the woodwork so common to old houses dating back to the Victorian Era.

Slowly, she backed away from the porch and took a second look. Quietly she said, "You're right, Grant. The woodwork is designed like spider webs. I wonder why?"

Grant gave an eerie laugh. "Because, Mimi—IT'S A FUNERAL HOME!"

Miss Emma sniffed. "Well, since we're here, you might as well take a look inside."

Christina looked at Grant and Grant stared back at his sister. No way were they going in a creepy, old place that once was filled with dead people!

Well, that's what they thought...before
Mimi turned to them. "Come on," she said.
"We might as well look."

4
FOR SALE: THE OLD MANSE

The door creaked loudly when Miss Emma opened it. It was strangely dim inside. She flicked a switch. "Power's been turned off," she remarked.

Mimi had to brush away real cobwebs to get into the hallway. Reluctantly, Christina and Grant followed. They wished that Papa had come along. Surely he would have made Mimi turn right around and go back home, NOT look at what obviously was totally unsuited for any kind of shop, much less a nice book shop.

Slowly, they paraded through the house, one behind the other. Miss Emma had little to say as she led them through a confusing maze of rooms. Most of what she said the kids didn't understand, but Mimi added to the commentary as they walked along:

Miss Emma: "Reception Parlor."

Mimi: "Where the deceased's family would have waited to be greeted by the staff."

Christina noted the faux marble fireplace, gold leaf decorations, and a curious stained-glass bat over the doorway. A large pump organ propped against one wall. But the real estate agent was moving rapidly and they followed close behind.

Miss Emma: "Viewing Room."

Mimi: "Where the family would come to see the body in the coffin they had chosen."

Miss Emma: "Cooling Room."

Mimi: (After a moment's hesitation...) "Where, uh, where they would have kept the bodies, uh, chilled, until they were, uh, embalmed."

Before Grant could ask what *embalmed* meant, Miss Emma led them into what sort of looked like a old-fashioned kitchen, only not so much so, even though it had a large stainless steel table and a big sink, plus a round drain in the floor as large as a dinner plate.

Miss Emma: "Embalming Room."

Mimi: (With much more hesitation...) "Uh, where the dead bodies had their internal fluids drained out, and, and, uh, stuff like that."

Now, Christina and Grant were both silent. They were trying hard not to throw up!

Next, Miss Emma led them into what looked like an old-fashioned bathroom only it was quite large for that. It had flowered curtains on the window, and a matching skirted dresser filled with silver trays of scissors, combs, brushes, compacts of powder, and many tubes of lipstick. A large claw-foot bathtub sat smackdab in the center of the room.

Miss Emma: "Make-up Room."

Mimi: "Where they 'fixed-up' the embalmed bodies so they looked real nice for the funeral."

The next room had closets all around. Several of the doors were open and they could see that some held long, dingy white dresses, or dusty, old-fashioned men's suits.

Miss Emma did not even comment. She just led them hastily through some other empty rooms—but not up the staircase to the second floor—and out the back door to the cemetery!

"I'll give you time to think," Miss Emma said, prissily, and pranced off as she slung open her cell phone to make a call. The kids followed Mimi as she wandered through the garden of gnarled wisteria, overgrown paths, and ancient tumbled tombstones, stained and moss-covered.

Mimi plodded all the way to the back of the property. Then she turned and stared at the enormous, rambling house with its rotted boards, peeling paint, tattered fish-scale roof shingles, and falling-down shutters over bay windows so dirty you could not see through them.

Suddenly, Mimi surprised the kids by prancing around the side of the house. The kids breathed a sigh of relief. They figured that was Mimi's way of saying "Thanks, but no thanks!" to Miss Emma, if she was watching. Both kids tossed their heads in the air haughtily and marched so close behind Mimi that they almost tumbled into her when she stopped short in front of the house.

Hands on hips, Mimi stared up at the house, then looked at her grandchildren, and shocked them by saying:

"It's perfect...JUST PERFECT!"

5
ONE SPOOKY PLACE

"PERFECT?" cried Grant. "PERFECT?! Mimi, it's a funeral home. Where dead people used to live, uh die, uh, get bombed, uh, whatever...are you kidding?"

"Mimi!" Christina pleaded. "It's nasty, gross. Did you see how dirty everything is? Mom would probably say it's contaminated, you know, with those yucky old body fluids you talked about. She would never let me and Grant help you..."

Mimi held up her hand for them to hush.

"It's all those things and more, I agree," Mimi said gently. "But let me paint another picture for you."

The kids stood there amazed and enthralled as their grandmother described how she saw the eventual shop:

"Imagine..." she began. "Imagine the front yard and fences all cleaned up and repaired and a perfect stone path to the shop, all quaint and prettily-painted with the gingerbread glistening and the veranda dripping in blooming wisteria.

"Imagine an inviting, double-front screened door with our sign overhead, the veranda with cushioned rocking chairs, perhaps even a rope hammock on the rounded end, where customers can sit and read and chat.

"Imagine a lovely reception area with a toasty fire in the winter, and that crystal chandelier glittering in the sunlight. I can just picture Christina welcoming customers, as well as taking their money for the large heaps of books they just can't live without!

"Imagine each room devoted to different kinds of books kids love to read, each room having its own unique design, furnishings, shelving, lights, and sitting areas.

Customers can wander at leisure from room to room, marveling at such an array of books as they never imagined.

"Imagine a lovely tea room, where customers can sit inside at quaint, little tables and chairs like you find at an ice cream parlor, or out in the garden among more paths, flowers, and fountains.

"Imagine..."

Suddenly, Grant held his hand up like a STOP SIGN and interrupted his grandmother, who was getting so carried away that her bright green eyes were glistening with tears.

"Enough, Mimi, please!" begged Grant. "Let me imagine for awhile, ok?"

With a frown, Mimi nodded and Grant continued:

"Imagine all the snakes in this yard, just waiting to greet customers and how they will like that, or spiders hiding in the eaves, just waiting to fall down on a strand of web into your customers' hair!

"Imagine how much money it's going to cost to fix up this joint and what Papa will say about that. Imagine all the rickety floors we just walked across and the screeching doors and what a racket that will make in your peaceful and quiet book shop.

"Imagine...just imagine...ghosts and bloodstains and body fluid smells that just won't go away, and being here at night all by yourself restocking the shelves, and..."

Now Christina interrupted her brother by doubling over with laughter.

"What's so funny?" grumbled Grant, hands on his hips. He glared at his sister.

Christina wiped a tear from her own eye. "I can sure tell who's gonna be the next writer in the family!" she said. "You know Mimi—with our help, of course—can get this place all fixed up just fine. It will be a very nice book shop, and tea room, and I can't wait!"

Grant frowned. "Well, I'm not pooh-poohing Mimi's idea," he said. He glanced at his grandmother, hoping he had not hurt her feelings, but he just had his own feelings about this place. "Whatever Mimi wants to do, I'm all for. I'm just sayin'..."

Now Mimi held up her STOP SIGN hand. "I hear you, Grant," she promised. "And I appreciate your concerns and, uh, warnings. But really, it will all be ok."

"So what do we do next?" asked Christina, clearly eager to embark on this exciting new venture.

Miss Emma answered that question by coming up the walk with a smug look on her face: "We go to the bank and get ready to close!"

Grant was puzzled. "Close? I thought we were going to open a shop, not close one."

"Oh, Grant, closing means when you sign all the legal documents to buy a piece of real estate," Christina said, then glanced at her grandmother to see if she was even halfway right.

Mimi nodded. "But first," she said, "we have to do something far scarier than anything Grant has brought up so far."

Startled, both kids asked together, "What, Mimi, what?"

Mimi shook her head and put on her worried face. She headed up the walk toward the golf cart. As she got in, she turned to them and said, "We have to go tell Papa!"

As Miss Emma and Christina climbed into the cart, Grant took one last glance back at the Old Manse Funeral Home. In spite of the warm sun, he felt a shiver go up his spine and all the way to his neck where it made the tiny hairs there stand on end. He didn't care what Mimi said—this was one spooky place.

6
THE CLOSING

Much to everyone's surprise, Papa was all for Mimi's "folly," as he called it.

"Sounds like a great idea!" he boomed. "Mimi likes to stay busy and this will be a challenging project, but she has you kids to help her, and me, of course."

"But, Papa..." Grant tried to say, but Papa went on, "Mimi has written so many books over the years, what a great place to sell them! And, Christina, I know you can help do a great design and decorating job, with your interest in architecture."

"Thank you, Papa," Christina said, beaming.

"But, Papa..." Grant tried to get his two-cents' worth in once more.

"And, Grant, you'll do a great job on the website where kids anywhere can go visit the shop online," Papa continued, ignoring Grant's eagerness to talk.

Before Grant could try again, Mimi said, "But what about the money?"

"No, problem!" said Papa. "Miss Emma texted me from the house, and I've already called the bank and arranged a loan. In fact, the closing is this very afternoon!" Papa looked proud of himself. He had certainly surprised Mimi, which was hard to do. Both kids looked stunned. Mimi was speechless—well, for a moment.

"Papa!" she screamed, giving him such a bear hug and big, fat kiss that she knocked his cowboy hat off his head and onto the floor. Papa didn't mind. "Thank you!"

For a moment, Mimi looked worried again. "I think it will be a good investment, but so soon? Do you think we need to think about it some more? Why, you haven't even seen the place!"

"That's right!" said Grant, who was completely ignored.

"I trust your intuition and judgment, Mimi," Papa said. "You take the kids and go to the closing. I am going to take a nap. Later, we'll take the Ladybug golf cart over to see your new book shop, and then go to dinner to celebrate!"

Grant surrendered. He slumped in a chair and put his head in his hands.

"Don't worry, buddy," Papa said, scrubbing his knuckles across Grant's hair as he headed for his office to take a nap.

Before Grant could reply, Miss Emma's golf cart horn tooted and Mimi and Christina went running. Reluctantly, Grant followed. He felt the same chill as he had at the house and hoped that one day someone would listen to *his* intuition for a change.

At the bank, which was only a few blocks away, all the paperwork was laid out on a large table like some giant school test.

Miss Emma sat at one end and had saved chairs for Mimi, Christina, and Grant. The banker sat at the other end. On one side of the table sat a lawyer. And on the other side sat an older woman who was there to be the witness.

Mimi said, "I'm glad you kids came to the closing with me. You can learn a little about business. After all, you may buy property some day. Fortunately, Mr. Manse didn't die intestate."

"He died on the interstate?" Grant said and wondered why his grandmother laughed, until she explained that *intestate* is when you die without a will.

The closing had sounded boring, and now, as they took their seats, it looked sort of scary, like they were on trial or something. Christina hoped it would not take very long. Grant wondered why the lawyer looked so grim.

The lawyer began, "I am the lawyer for the Maynard Manse estate. As far as I have been able to ascertain, there is no living survivor. The old Manse property represents the last thing Mr. Manse owned that needs to be liquidated."

The lawyer took a deep breath and paused, while Grant wondered what *ascertained* meant and if *liquidate* meant the house would flood. It all sounded very legal-schmegal to him.

Finally, the lawyer added, "Mr. Manse's will says that the property must be sold 'as is,' including all outbuildings, furnishings, and, well, anything else that was left behind at the time of his death."

Christina and Grant exchanged glances. On the one hand, that sounded exciting; they had spotted some pretty cool things in the house during the short time they had been inside, and they hadn't even gone upstairs. On the other hand, Mr. Manse was a funeral home operator—maybe he had left behind some things they didn't want.

Mimi said, "I understand."

The banker whipped out a hand full of black pens faster than you could say "geehawwhimmydiddle" and passed them around. Soon a flurry of papers to sign passed from Mimi to the lawyer to the banker to the witness and all you could hear was the scrub of pen on paper.

At last there was a neat, tidy stack of paper in front of the witness lady, who jumped up and ran to make copies of the signed documents for everyone.

Miss Emma cleared her throat. "While we're waiting, I might as well go ahead and give you this," she said cheerily, sliding a small black box across the table to Mimi.

Mimi was beaming. She had just bought her first piece of commercial property—her soon-to-be book shop. "What is it?" she asked, reaching for the black box and opening it.

Suddenly, her smile turned to a frown. "Hmm, Grant, I think this might interest you?" She slid the box toward her grandson.

Nervously, Grant took the box and opened it for himself.

"What is it, Grant?" Christina asked, straining to see inside the ancient box that appeared to be made of old leather and lined with black silk.

"Oh, for heaven's sake!" muttered Miss Emma. "It's just the door key to the house, ya'll."

Slowly, Grant pulled the key out of the box and held it up for all to see. "Yeah," said Grant. "A SKELETON key!"

7

A PIG IN A POKE?

"Oh, dear, what have I done?!" Mimi wailed, after the closing was over and she had taken the kids to an ice cream shop to "celebrate."

"Aw, don't be discouraged, Mimi," said Grant. "It's just an old skeleton key. A lot of old houses opened with these old, iron keys."

"They aren't very secure," said Christina. "I'm sure Papa will want to replace the lock this key goes in with a deadbolt."

"DEADbolt!" wailed Mimi. "Oh, what have I done?!"

Christina and Grant laughed.

Mimi finally laughed, too. "I guess I just have cold feet," she admitted. "It's a big deal to buy a piece of property and start a new business. I think I have a case of nerves. Or," she pondered, "have I bought a pig in a poke?"

"What's that?" asked Grant, licking his root beer ice cream cone. "I thought you bought a funeral home, not a hog farm."

"Don't be silly, silly!" said Christina. She was slurping a key lime milkshake through a straw. "Mimi means maybe she bought something that she did not exactly know what it was, right, Mimi?"

Mimi nodded sadly. "Alas, yes," she said, then perked right up. "But it's been done and now it's time to make my dream come true. Maybe we should go see my new pig in a poke and see if that skeleton key actually opens the door. What do you think, kids?"

Grant glanced outside. "It's getting late, Mimi. Are you sure you want to be over there if it gets dark?"

Mimi glanced at her watch. "If we hurry, we'll have plenty of time to explore the property a little more before it gets dark. After all, we didn't get to all the rooms, especially not the basement and the attic."

"Basement?" said Christina.

"Attic?" said Grant.

"Yeah!" said Mimi. "Oh, boy, hey?!" She hopped up and scooped up their trash to discard.

As she headed to the garbage can in the corner, Christina and Grant looked at each other and said, "Oh, brother!"

By the time they ran by to get Papa and sped out to the Manse house, it was indeed dusk. At least it was cooler, but not much. As they pulled up at the funeral home, lightning bugs flickered in the kudzu vines.

"No worries!" said Papa, hopping out of the car. "I brought candles, matches, and flashlights!"

"Surely there's electricity?" Mimi said hopefully. "I thought the bulbs were just burned out earlier."

"No one's been in here forever," Papa reminded her. "I'm pretty sure no one's been paying any utility bills." Papa shoved the skeleton key into the old door lock and the door creaked open. "Mmm, mmm," Papa said, shaking his head. "Gotta get some deadbolt locks for these doors right away!"

Christina and Grant giggled, then followed Mimi and Papa into the dim, fading afternoon light of the parlor.

"Nice, Mimi," said Papa. "A real jewel you bought here. Or, maybe, just maybe, a pig in a poke?"

Now, Mimi really did wail. "Oh, Papa, please don't say that! I'm sure this old place will make a lovely book shop. All the way over I was trying to think of what to name it. Now, you've teased me and made me worry and made me..."

It was clear what Papa had made Mimi do: CRY!

As Mimi plopped in a dusty chair and put her head in her hands, Papa shook his head and handed the kids his bag of flashlights and candles and matches. "You guys take a gander, while I comfort Mimi. We'll be right behind you."

Once more, Christina and her brother giggled. They knew that Papa would set things right, probably by promising Mimi enough money to get the whole "joint," as Grant called it, fixed up in fine style. Mimi always did everything first-class after all.

"Come, on, Christina!" Grant said, hurrying through the rooms they'd seen the other day. "Let's check out the basement and attic on our own, before it gets any darker."

"Not afraid are you, little brother?" Christina teased.

"NO!" said Grant. "It's just an old, beat-up Victorian house that was once a funeral home—what's there to be afraid of?"

About that time, Grant whooshed through a doorway covered in cobwebs that slathered his hair. "Yikes!" he said, but pressed on. Then he slowed down, way down.

"What's wrong?" asked Christina.

"Papa put the skeleton key in the bag, too," said Grant. "I was feeling for the flashlight, but I grabbed the key instead."

"So, what?" said Christina.

"There's a tag hanging on it," Grant said.

"Like I said, so what?!" Christina repeated. "It's just the address of this place, I guess."

Grant pulled her over to one of the dusky windows to look and see. It was a piece of brown, crackly paper, folded in half. It hung on the key by a thin red thread. Together they tugged the dry, brittle tag open. Together they read:

> NOW WHAT HAVE YOU DONE?
> IT'S NOT YOURS TO OWN...
> THE PLACE WHERE YOU STAND...
> HAS LONG BEEN MY HOME.

"Oh, dear," said Christina. "Who in the world wrote this?" She looked closer at the handwriting, which was in ink, but faded from black to light gray. The writing was very scrawled, as if by a child or an old person with arthritic hands, perhaps. "It sure sounds like a warning to me!"

Grant cackled. "Oh, Christina, poor sister, this is NOT a warning," he said. "This, this, this, dear sister, is a CLUE!"

Christina groaned. "A clue? A clue to what?"

Now, Grant gave her a throaty, spooky, deep, frightening laugh. "Look around!" he said, spreading his arms wide, stirring up more dust and cobwebs. "What do you see?"

Christina stared into the dimness. "A dirty, old house," she said.

"No," insisted Grant. "What you see is MYSTERY! Rooms and rooms and rooms of it! I don't know if who wrote this clue is alive...or dead...but I don't think they want to scare us off. I think they want us to find them!"

"Well, guess what, little brother," Christina said, stomping off. "I don't want to find anyone in this old place—dead or alive. I'm getting out of here!"

As Christina turned to head back to the parlor to find Mimi and Papa, she started for the last door they had come through. But before she could get to it—it slammed shut!

8
WHO DAT?

Christina and Grant both screamed. Suddenly the door sprung back open and a figure loomed in the doorway, large and dark. It boomed, "WHO DAT?!"

"Papa!" cried Christina. "You about scared us to death!"

"Didn't mean to," said Papa. "I just came to tell you Mimi say's it's too dark to explore tonight, after all. We'll come back in the morning—with brooms and mops, and such."

"And help, too?" Christina asked. "This will be a big job."

"We could bring Avery, Ella, and Evan," Grant suggested, glad it was dark, so they couldn't see his knees wobbling.

"And maybe a couple of our friends?" said Christina, eager to show her friends this wild and crazy place before it got all cleaned up.

"Sure!" said Papa. "We'll need all the help we can get. You know Mimi won't want to waste any time getting this place fixed up and ready to open."

It was quiet for a moment as they stood in the darkness. "Papa?" Grant finally said.

"Uh, Grant," Christina interrupted. "I think Papa wants us to leave, so don't bother him with questions right now."

Grant knew that Christina was afraid he'd tell Papa about the clue, but he wouldn't. Mystery-solving was what he and Christina did. Besides, the clue would just worry Mimi, and she might change her mind and re-sell this place, just when this place was getting very interesting.

"I just wondered if Mimi did buy a pig in a poke?" Grant said, much to his sister's relief.

Papa laughed and shoved his grandkids back through the darkness toward the parlor. "I don't know about a pig in a poke," he said.

"Maybe a corpse in a coffin? Or a ghost in the garage? Or a..."

"PAPA!" both kids squealed.

"Just kidding!" said Papa, with a laugh. "Just kidding."

But as Christina and Grant wandered back through the cooling room, and the viewing room, and the embalming room to the parlor, they wondered. They really, really wondered.

9
SATURDAY

The next day was sunny and much cooler. Bright and early, they were all over at what they now called "The Shop."

The cleaning crew included Mimi, Papa, Christina, and Grant; cousins Avery, Ella, and little Evan; Christina and Grant's mom and dad; Uncle Michael and Aunt Cassidy; plus Christina's friend McKenzie and Grant's friend Thomas.

They all stood in the front yard, sorting out rags, brooms, mops, and other cleaning and gardening tools. There was lots of chatter about the house and some excitement about new discoveries: a small vine-covered chapel for "services," a gazebo at one end of the yard, and an old-brick carriage house or tool shed (no one knew) in the far corner of the property.

"Lots to do!" said the adults.

"Lots to explore!" cheered the kids.

Just as they were about to head to their assigned duties, a golf cart screeched down the drive and Miss Emma hopped out.

"Hi, ya'll!" she said, marching right up to Mimi. "Forgot to give you this at the closing. Well, actually, I didn't give it to you because the lawyer forgot to give it to me." She handed Mimi a square leather box.

Mimi looked at it suspiciously. "No more skeleton keys, I hope?"

Miss Emma giggled. "No! This is something good. It's a diary! Mr. Manse kept a diary for almost one hundred years. He was really old when he died, you know. It was part of his estate, so it belongs to you."

Mimi opened the box and sure enough, there was an old, dusty, thick leather-bound book filled with pages and pages of writing.

Mimi nodded and closed the book and the box back up, but Christina could see her eyes gleam. She knew her grandmother could hardly wait to take the diary someplace private and begin to read it. "Thank you," Mimi said.

Miss Emma nodded and hopped back on her golf cart. Tootle-loo!" she cried, and with a wave over her shoulder, sped off. "Have fun!"

The rest of the adults had already headed off to begin work. Mimi made a beeline to the gazebo, the diary tucked beneath her arm. As Christina and Grant rounded up the rest of the kids, Grant whispered to his sister, "Did you see the writing in the diary?"

"Sure did!" said Christina. "The same writing as the clue, I think."

Grant snickered. "Told you it was a clue!"

"Yeah," said Christina, handing out dust cloths. "I heard you. But have you also heard: Mr. Manse is dead, been dead. So how did he write that tag?"

Christina led the kids off to dust and sweep. Grant lingered in the yard beneath the massive magnolia tree, gray beads of Spanish moss tickling the back of his sweaty neck.

"Good question," he whispered to himself. "Good question."

It was a busy day!

Dad and Uncle Mike tackled the yard work.

Mom and Aunt Cassidy cleaned the embalming room/kitchen for the tea room.

Avery and Ella swept and dusted all the downstairs rooms.

Christina and McKenzie bravely tackled the attic.

Grant and Thomas reluctantly descended to the basement.

Papa cleaned in the chapel.

Mimi sat in an old wicker rocker in the shabby gazebo and read *The Manse Diary*. The more she read, the bigger her eyes got!

10
THE ATTIC

"Christina, I don't think I'd have agreed to come and help if I'd known we'd be stuck up in some spooky, dark, cobwebby old attic," grumbled McKenzie, as she ascended the narrow staircase that creaked with each step.

"Oh, don't be so chicken-livered," said Christina. "I wanted to do the attic. No one's probably been up here in a hundred years—no telling what valuable antiques or jewelry or other stuff we might find!"

Christina led the way, a bucket of cleaning supplies in one hand and a large flashlight in the other.

"Yeah," said McKenzie, as they continued to climb. "But you said this was an old funeral home, so we might also find dead bodies, or who knows what up here."

Suddenly, Christina tripped on the top step and fell face first onto the attic floor. A flurry of dust stirred up into a cloud, each mote glittering from sunlight that filtered in through the slatted, wooden air vents on each end of the attic.

Christina stood up and brushed off her knees. She reached behind her and helped her friend up into the attic. They both slowly turned around in a circle to see what they could see.

"Wow!" said McKenzie. "It's a really big attic! It must cover the entire house and you can stand up, not like in my attic at home, where you have to crawl around."

"Yes," said Christina. "Only the house must be a lot bigger than I thought. I know we didn't get to all the rooms downstairs yet, and this place really rambles, but this is the biggest attic I've ever seen!"

"You can't even see into all the dark corners," fretted McKenzie.

"True," Christina agreed, "but look at all this stuff!"

The girls made one more turn to stare in amazement at all the crates, trunks, storage boxes, bookcases, display cases, barrels, and many other containers, some spilling over with fabrics, glass bottles and jars, and many other things.

Christina sighed. "I don't even know where to begin!"

"How about by turning on that flashlight," said McKenzie.

Christina nodded and punched the ON button. At first nothing happened, then the light burst brightly toward a far corner of the attic.

Both girls jumped at the skeleton that suddenly came into view! They squealed involuntarily and grabbed each other, holding on for dear life.

"I don't think it's a real skeleton," Christina said, her voice quivering. "See, it's on a stand, like we have in biology class."

McKenzie released her grip on her friend's arm. "Well, it could still be a real skeleton, but I see what you mean. Let's go check it out!"

Before Christina could object, her suddenly brave friend took off on a zigzagged path through all the crates and cartons to reach that corner of the attic. They stirred up so much dust that by the time they reached the skeleton, both girls were coughing and sneezing.

"Hey, look!" said McKenzie. "He's wearing a nametag."

Christina giggled. "That's silly! So what's his name?" she asked peering in the dim light to try to read the pale writing.

"I don't care what it is," said McKenzie, "let's call him Bone-a-part, ok?"

"Sure," said Christina. "Why not? Mimi will probably love to have a mascot skeleton for the shop, named Bone-a-part. After all, she has a mummy at the door to her office."

"What?" asked McKenzie, with a gasp.

"Sure," said Christina. "Haven't you seen it? It's cool. It has a horn tied to it that says, 'Toot 'n' come in'!"

"Huh?" said McKenzie.

"It's an Egyptian mummy," said Christina, with a giggle, "think about it!"

While McKenzie pondered this pun/riddle, Christina's vision had finally adjusted enough to read the nametag stuck to the skeleton's ribs. "Uh, oh..."

"What is it?!" McKenzie asked. "It is just a biology skeleton, right?"

"I guess," said Christina, "but that's not the problem. It's not a nametag. It's written by the same person who wrote the tag on the skeleton key that opens the house."

"Well, what does it say?" McKenzie asked.

Christina began to read,

YOU GOT THIS FAR
NOW GO BACK
OR BE PREPARED
FOR AN ATTIC ATTACK.

McKenzie gasped. "Then maybe we'd better heed that warning and get out of here! Skeletons, mummies, this place gives me the creeps. I don't think your grandmother needs this space for her shop, anyway. It's too big."

Christina did not respond. Slowly, she peeled the label from the skeleton's ribs. "Another clue," she muttered to herself.

"A what?" said McKenzie. "A clue? What are you talking about?"

"Mystery," said Christina. "A real mystery!"

To her surprise, McKenzie stomped off. "Clues! Mystery! What is it with you and your brother? How many clues and how many mysteries can you and your family ever be involved in? It's crazy!"

As McKenzie stomped back down the stairs, Christina followed, but took one more spin around. "I *will* come back," she whispered. "I will see what's in all these boxes. I will find some kind of treasure. I just feel it in my...my bones!"

11
THE BASEMENT

Grant and Thomas had headed for the basement. A curved set of brick stairs went around and down to the lowest level of the house from a room they had not been in before.

"I'm not a big fan of basements," said Thomas as he clumped down the steps behind Grant.

"Me, either," said Grant, "but the choices around this joint aren't all that wonderful. It's bad or badder. Maybe the basement won't be as awful as we think."

But it was. Like the attic, the basement seemed to extend beneath the entire house, the original part as well as the many rooms added for the funeral home.

A dozen small-screened vent windows dotted the upper perimeter wall of the basement. The small amount of light they provided helped the boys see anything at all.

As far as Grant and Thomas could see, there were crates, barrels, boxes, and heaps and stacks of unknown stuff.

"It sure smells dank and damp down here," complained Thomas. "I hope there aren't any mice."

"Or rats!" added Grant, the thought of which stopped both boys in their tracks.

"This entire place seems to grow cobwebs," Grant groused, swiping a snarl of gray, cotton candy-like webs from the top of his ball cap. "I don't think anyone has been down here in forever."

"Well, nobody *living*," teased Thomas.

"Don't even talk about it!" said Grant.

The boys slowly walked the narrow path left between all the stuff in the basement, poking now and then at a box.

"Not the usual garden tools, and such," said Thomas.

"I guess those things are out in that tool shed building," said Grant. "This stuff seems to be more related to, uh, you know—funeral stuff."

"Like what?" Thomas asked warily.

Grant plucked a test tube and beaker from an open crate. "Like this scientific-looking stuff. Seems like these kinds of things might have been used in the embalming room, maybe?"

"What's embalming?" asked Thomas.

Grant shrugged. "You don't want to know."

"Are we supposed to clean?" Thomas asked.

"Thank goodness, no," said Grant. "Papa said just look around and report back how bad it is down here."

"Well, I think we know the answer to that," said Thomas, weaving further into the mass of boxes. "But what is this?"

Grant waded over to where his friend was looking at a large barrel. A square of paper was taped to the top. Grant figured it must be a list of the contents of the barrel, but he was mistaken.

As he bent over to read the label, he recognized the same handwriting he had seen on the skeleton key tag. He read aloud:

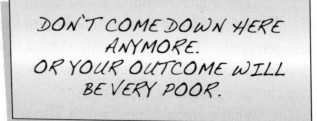

DON'T COME DOWN HERE ANYMORE.
OR YOUR OUTCOME WILL BE VERY POOR.

Thomas was astounded. "Who could have written that?" he asked. "And how long ago? And why? Who did they expect to read it?"

Slowly, Grant looked around the basement. At the far corner, he spied one of the small, narrow windows that let light and ventilation into the basement. Only this window had no screen; it was open to the back yard of the house.

"Might not have been so long ago," he said quietly. "I have no idea who wrote it, but I am afraid it might have been written for us, well, Mimi, our family. I don't think someone wants Mimi to open a book shop here."

Carefully, Grant ripped off the paper, folded it, and stuck it in the back pocket of his cargo shorts. "Come on," he told Thomas, tugging at his tee shirt. "Let's get out of here."

As quickly as they could, the boys wound their way back to the brick steps and up to the large wooden trapdoor. But the door would not budge. They could not get out!

12

LUNCH BUNCH

By noon, everyone was dirty, sweaty, hot, exhausted, and starving. Slowly, by ones and twos, the work gang trickled toward the shady gazebo where Aunt Cassidy had unpacked her oversized picnic hamper.

She spread a red-and-white checkered cloth on a round table and set out plates of fried chicken, potato salad, sliced tomatoes, bread and butter pickles, ham sandwiches, peanut butter cookies, and pitchers of cold lemonade.

"Yum!" said McKenzie, going for a paper plate. "Don't mind if I do!"

Mimi and Mom followed her in line, as the men crowded right behind.

"I'm hungrier than a...than a...than a..." Papa began, rubbing his tummy, which was covered by a now very dirty tee shirt. "Well, I don't know what I'm hungrier than," he muttered, fanning himself with his paper plate, "but I am!"

Just then his tummy growled as loud as a foghorn and everyone laughed.

Aunt Cassidy gathered up Avery, Ella, and Evan and made them a picnic on a blanket on the ground.

"Christina, aren't you hungry?" asked Mimi.

Christina hung back near the back door of the house. "Uh, I'm just wondering what's keeping Grant and Thomas," she said. "Grant's usually first in line for food, you know."

Her dad nodded. "Yep, but maybe he and Thomas just want to finish what they are doing. Come on and eat; they'll show up sooner or later."

Christina hesitated. She didn't want to eat. What she wanted to do was to show Grant the clue she had found and see if he had found one, as well. But her dad was still looking at her so she knew she'd better mind and get in line.

Before long, everyone was eating and talking and laughing. Evan fell asleep on the blanket and Papa leaned against a tree and nodded off. It seemed everyone thought that if they kept on eating and chatting, the rest of the hard work at hand would wait. Maybe it would, but Mimi wouldn't.

"Hey, you guys, you don't fool me!" she teased. I know it's hot and everyone has worked hard, but there's still so much to do. We need to finish up and get back to work, please." Mimi downed the rest of her iced tea and began to clean up.

"Mimi, don't forget about Grant and Thomas before we put all the food away," said Christina. She kept an eye on the back door and hurried to finish her lunch so she could go look for them.

Her dad popped his head up from the book he was reading. "Those boys haven't shown up yet?" He looked worried and jumped up and headed for the house. "Where were they working, Christina?"

"The basement," she answered, scrambling after him. McKenzie followed.

They traipsed quickly through the maze of rooms to the room where they saw the trapdoor to the basement closed snug.

"Well, they must have gotten done and gone off to play," her dad guessed.

As they turned to leave, Christina heard a *thump thump thump*. "Dad! That sound is coming from down below!"

He spun around and reached for the big iron circle you pulled to open the door. Beneath them, he could hear muffled shouts. At last, he tugged open the heavy door.

Grant and Thomas bounded out in a huff. "Thank goodness!" said Grant. "I thought we were going to be down there forever. Someone locked us in, Dad!"

His father laughed. "No they didn't, Grant. The door just stuck. It's old and out of kilter, so it must have slammed behind you and just stuck harder than you boys could push."

Grant looked doubtful. He shoved cobwebs from his face and gave Christina a look. "Well, we're starving!" he said.

"Then head to the backyard," ordered his father, "before they put all the food away.

Drink plenty of liquid and take a rest before you get back to work."

As their father headed off, Thomas followed McKenzie, but Christina and Grant lagged behind.

"Did you find a clue?" Grant asked breathlessly.

"Sure did," said Christina, tossing her arm around her brother's quivering shoulders. She could tell he was pretty shook up.

"Me, too!" said Grant. "I think we need to eat and have a confab."

"A what?" Christina said.

"A confab, you know, a talk about what the dickens is going on here," her brother answered. "I know we like to solve mysteries on our own, but I don't want to get stuck anywhere in this creepy old house again, do you hear me."

"I hear you," Christina promised, as she propelled him out the back door and toward the gazebo on his wobbly legs. "Don't worry—we'll figure it out. I sure don't want to do all this dadgum cleaning for nothing!"

"What do you mean?" asked Grant.

"I mean if something bad's going on, and Mimi chickens out on her book shop idea," Christina explained, "I sure would rather it be before we get this place spic and span."

"Surely she won't chicken out!" Grant said.

"Probably not," said Christina, well aware of how stubborn and determined her grandmother was. But she also knew how she had felt when she found the clue in the attic. "But *we* might chicken out, Grant. *We* might."

13
CONFAB IN THE GAZEBO

After lunch, Aunt Cassidy took Avery, Ella, and Evan home. Mom and Dad and Mimi went inside to work on the upstairs rooms in the house. Uncle Michael said he would weed the tombstone garden. And Papa took a nap in the hammock near the brick tool shed. "Can't help myself," he'd said with a big yawn.

Under the guise of "working on the design of the shop," Christina, Grant, Thomas, and McKenzie gathered in the gazebo with the rest of the lemonade, peanut butter cookies— and the clues—for their confab.

"What do you think is going on?" asked Thomas. "You and Christina are pretty experienced in this mystery-solving thing," he added, pointing to Grant. "So do you think this is a real mystery, or are you just overreacting?"

McKenzie frowned. "The clues are REAL, Thomas. And they each sound so much like a threat and a warning to get away from here and never come back. Christina and Grant aren't making that up!"

They all sat criss-cross-applesauce in the center of the old, six-sided gazebo, beneath a wooden paddle fan moving lazily through the thick air.

"Oh, someone is definitely trying to scare Mimi off!" said Christina. "And I think they are alive—not dead. I don't really believe in ghosts, you know. But we just don't have enough information to go on. We've either got to find more clues or try to get the perp to show his, or her, hand."

"The perp?" said McKenzie.

"The perpetrator," Grant explained. "The person behind the clues and threats and warnings."

"But except for Miss Emma, we haven't met anyone associated with the house," said Thomas.

"Not yet!" said Grant. He looked at his sister. "But we need to ferret them out, right?"

Christina tossed her brother the last cookie. "Right, Grant. The hard thing is that they are obviously nowhere around here. So do they have an accomplice? Did Mr. Manse plant the clues long before he died, just to scare anyone away from this place? Or does someone else have an ulterior motive?"

"Like maybe they want this place for themselves?" guessed Grant.

Thomas frowned. "How many people can get excited about owning a creepy old funeral home besides your grandmother?" he said, then blushed. "Uh, sorry—no offense."

"None taken," Christina assured him. "There are only two immediate problems," she added thoughtfully, running her finger around the dust in the center of the gazebo floor until she had drawn a large question mark.

"What problems?" McKenzie asked warily.

"First," said Christina, "we need to meet some more possible candidates for the BD."

"Bad Guy," Grant translated.

"Even if some are actually RH's," Christina added.

"Red Herrings," said Grant.

"And find some more CC's," said Christina.

"Creepy Clues," Grant explained.

"And not RG's," Christina finished.

When Grant hesitated, McKenzie and Thomas looked at him eagerly.

Christina nudged her brother with her shoulder. "The things Grant does believe in..." she hinted.

Grant shuddered. "Real Ghosts!"

For a moment the other kids were silent. Then Thomas muttered, "If there are RG's, then this is surely the kind of place they might hang out."

They all stared at the house. A dark cloud passed overhead, turning the entire scene before them gray and gloomy. Suddenly, they heard a loud "BOO!" behind them and turned to see Papa, up from his nap, hair mussed.

"Got your attention!" he teased. "Why all the worried faces? We'll get this place fixed up in time. In fact, Mimi and I are taking a bunch of trash to the dump. Will you kids be ok here by yourselves till we get back? Won't be long at all."

"Where are Dad and Uncle Michael?" asked Christina, not crazy about being left behind. Once Mimi and Papa went off, you just never knew when they'd be back.

"Oh, they already left with a load of garbage," said Papa. "But they aren't coming back tonight. Your dad has to do some work and Uncle Michael has to take Avery to a sleepover."

With a giant yawn, Papa waved and strutted off. Soon they heard an engine rev and the trailer of trash rumble loudly as the car bounced down the driveway.

"Ok!" said Christina. "This is our chance!"

"Our chance to what?" the other kids asked together.

"Split up and get some work done!" Christina answered. She stood up and brushed off the back of her shorts. "If we split up, we can explore the whole house, top to bottom, and the outbuildings, too, until we ferret out any more clues!"

"You mean go...by ourselves?" asked McKenzie.

Grant laughed. He hung his fingers in front of her face and jiggled them, hissing *"Whoooooo...whoooooo...*not afraid are you?"

McKenzie slapped his hands away. "NO!" she insisted. But all the kids glanced at the house. The looks on their faces revealed how they really felt. Still, there was a mystery to be solved, and the sooner the better, they knew. And maybe even the safer.

Or, maybe not?

14
THE SEARCH

Christina dished out the orders, as usual:

"Thomas, you return to the basement, only this time put a stick under the door so it won't close. If you and Grant found one clue, there may be more.

"McKenzie, you go back up to the attic. It wasn't *that* scary. See if we overlooked any clues.

"Grant, you look at all the second floor rooms—we haven't even been up there, but Mimi and Aunt Cassidy cleaned up there, so it can't be too spooky. See if you find any clues, anything at all."

"And just what do you plan to do, big sister?" Grant asked.

"Sit here and drink lemonade and wait for our return?" He had his hands on his hips and his face up to her face.

"No, Grant, of course not, silly," she said, gently shoving him away. "I'm going to search all the rooms on the main level. Those ARE the scary rooms—embalming, coffins, making dead people look pretty, stuff like that!"

Christina glanced at her watch. "Let's each take just one hour then meet back here. If you run into any problem, just holler—oh, I don't know—GERONIMO!"

"GERONIMO?" the other three kids said.

Christina blushed and shrugged her shoulders. "Sure, why not? That's a good word to scream and we'll know what it means."

"You will?" asked Grant.

"Well, we'll know you've found something important, or run into a problem, that's what I mean, and we can all come running," said Christina.

"What KIND of problems?" Thomas asked nervously.

For a moment, all four kids froze in place and stared up at the house. It looked eerie and ominous in the fading afternoon light.

"We'll know them when we meet them," Christina said, then ran toward the house while she still had the courage. Reluctantly, the other kids followed...at a much slower pace.

Thomas dashed to the basement, not forgetting the stick and a large flashlight.

McKenzie bounded up the steps to the attic, also taking a flashlight and a baseball bat she had found on the back porch.

Grant trudged up to the second floor. He never thought to take anything. He just felt like he was headed to his doom.

Christina ran around the house and started at the front door. Her strategy was to pretend that she was Mr. Manse and see what could be of value that would make someone want to scare off others so they could keep this old place to themselves.

15
INDOORS, OUTDOORS

While the kids had gathered in the gazebo, all the real action had been taking place inside the Old Manse house. Perhaps someone watching would have noticed, or perhaps no one would have seen anything.

Either way, a keen eye might have spotted ventilation slats in the attic moving, and not from the wind...screens flapping from some of the high basement windows...doors, trapdoors, secret passages and more (most yet undiscovered by the children) being traversed by someone eager to get their subversive work done while the house was otherwise empty.

This someone well knew their way around the old funeral home, but by the time the children had come back inside to do their searches, this *someone was no longer to be seen or found, which is just the way they wanted it!*

16
A CLUE GOLDMINE

THOMAS: In the basement, Thomas decided to race through the maze of paths and look left and right, up and down as fast as he could for any clues. He hoped not to see anything scary, evil, ugly, or gross. He even thought maybe he would try to find a new friend, one who did not seem to live such a mysterious life.

For a while, it seemed all he stirred up was dust on the floor as he scooted past the heaps and mounds of stored stuff, whatever it was—and he was pretty sure he did not want to know what it was.

After a respectable search, he turned to head back and report. It was then that he noticed many of the small screens that once had been snug in the basement windows either tattered, torn, or flapping loose as if someone had just yanked them down at random or stirred them up as they flew in and out of the basement on some urgent errand.

Curious, Thomas bravely decided to walk the perimeter of the basement. Because many bags and sacks were stacked against the wall, he had to nudge or outright shove the lumpy parcels out of his path.

As he came to each window, it was easy to look down and see that he had indeed found a new clue—actually, new clues—one beneath each window! He did not bother to stop and read them, but just gathered them up as fast as he could and headed—also as fast as he could— to the stairs, breathless, and relieved to find that the stick had held the basement trapdoor open.

He shoved hard with one hand, the clues grasped in his other quivering hand, and made a dash for the backyard.

MCKENZIE: At the bottom of the attic stairs, McKenzie hesitated. She absolutely, positively did not want to go back up there. But Christina was always so brave, she thought, and she didn't want to disappoint her friend. Still, it was no fun to be sent on such a spooky assignment all alone, and the attic was already darker since the sun was going down.

McKenzie decided to stand at the doorway of the attic and stare, until her eyes adjusted to the lack of light, and to see all she could see without actually entering what she thought of as the inner sanctum of the scary.

She soon realized that this tactic was not going to work, so with a tremulous sigh, she stepped into the attic and began to retrace all the places she and Christina had searched earlier.

That was impossible, of course, since the path was such a helter-skelter pattern, like a maze you could walk over and over and never go the same way. Like Thomas, she thought speed was called for, and so she hurried as fast as she could, also looking up and down, left and right to spy any clue—without spying anything that might have to do with the fact that this was once a funeral home.

By the time she reached the other end of the attic, McKenzie realized she was so stressed that she was clenching her arms tight against her and her front teeth were clamped down on her lower lip.

She sighed, shook her arms to loosen them up, and rubbed her lip. With a fast spin on her heels, she turned to head back to the attic door. It was then that she disturbed one tall bundle, wrapped in burlap and tied with twine. The general shape of the bundle could only be described as that of a mummy.

As the bundle rocked to and fro toward and away from her, a small trunk behind it was overturned and crashed down at her feet.

With a squeal, McKenzie jumped back, then stared at the floor. She found herself standing in a puddle of notes, written in that peculiar handwriting—the notes that Christina called clues. She grabbed them up and ran for the door!

GRANT: In a very short time, Grant grew bored with the second floor. It was a big area, no doubt, but it was just one large, medium, or small empty room after the other. It was sort of mazelike with no organized pattern. He thought Mimi could make a lot of "book rooms" up here. But he was disappointed that there were no clues to be seen.

"At least it doesn't feel so scary," Grant muttered aloud to himself.

He couldn't be sure he had been in all the upstairs rooms, since it was such a maze, and it seemed odd that there were no closets or bathrooms. It made him wonder what this part of the house had been used for when it was a funeral home, but he guessed he didn't really want to know.

Bored, tired, thirsty, and wondering what to do next, Grant leaned against a wall to think. When he did, the wall first shuddered, then moved! As Grant froze in place, the wall turned, taking him with it!

The other side of the wall seemed to be just another room, smaller and darker. Grant had held his breath through the entire ordeal and now exhaled loudly. Quickly, he scooted across the room to get away from whatever mechanism he had activated to make the wall turn. Then again, he thought, maybe he needed the wall to move him back to where he came from?

Thinking hard, and nervous, he propped one hand against the far wall and, instantly, it fell open, revealing a secret spiral staircase. Grant held on for dear life, not wanting anything to close behind him again and leave him even further stranded and lost.

He peered down the staircase, but since it was spiral, he could not see the bottom. "Not going down there!" he said to himself. Quickly, he ran back to the other wall and patted his hands frantically to try to make it open. Just as he was about to give up, the wall spun around and spit him back out into the room he had come from.

Grant made a mad dash for the stairs and ran as fast as he could to find the others.

CHRISTINA: On the first floor, Christina made her way methodically from room to room. As quickly as possible she passed through the rooms they had been in often by now. They were still creepy to her, but clean now and the last light through the sparkling windows made it feel more like a real house and less like a creepy old funeral home.

As she entered the first "new" room, Christina slowed down. The rest of the downstairs rooms were dark, wood-paneled, and had a lot of elaborate built-in bookcases—perfect for a book shop, she thought.

Some rooms had heavy damask curtains tied back with thick-braided gold tassels over thin, dingy sheers which made Christina feel as if she had come through a time machine to the past.

At least there were no creepy packages, bundles, boxes, and not too many cobwebs. Still, it was scary to be so far into the unknown part of the house all alone.

Finally, there seemed to be no place else to go except through a heavy door. Cobwebs clotted the lock, so she could see that the room had not been entered in a very long time. Nor could she enter it—it was locked!

Christina remembered that she had opened the front door that morning. She searched her pockets and found the skeleton key. Nervously, she stuck the key into the lock. It turned easily and the door creaked open.

Fearful, Christina peered inside. At first she breathed a sigh of relief. "It's just an office," she said. But when she entered the room, she screeched! Enormous heads and eyes stared down at her from the wall.

As her eyes adjusted to the dim light, Christina saw that they were the stuffed and mounted heads of deer and other wild animals. She did not mind them so much, except for all those glistening eyes staring down at her as if to say, "What are you doing here?" Christina wondered the same thing herself.

She poked around the top of the large, ornate desk. "Mimi would love to write on this," she said aloud. There were more of Mr. Manse's journals, an old iron inkstand, and loads of green-lined ledgers, probably recounting the money made from his funeral home operations. There was also a yellowed notepad with writing on it.

Christina could see that the writing was the same, or at least very similar, to what was on the clues. She turned the notepad toward her, but it did not seem to be a clue. In the big, fat scrawl, it read:

Must get will changed.

Not much time.

Hope that Wilb...

And the writing stopped. Had Mr. Manse been interrupted, Christina wondered. Then she felt a cold chill and had a bad thought—or had he fallen over dead at this desk, perhaps from a heart attack, and never finished the note, or changed his will? And who, she worried, was Wilb?

Suddenly, Christina heard a noise. Maybe it was a mouse, she didn't know. But she was only so brave. Christina turned and ran back through the house to find the others.

17
CONFABBING AGAIN

By the time Christina reached the gazebo, it was almost dark. The other kids were already there, reading through the clues, arguing, and she startled them when she ran up and yelled, "Hey!"

"Yikes!" the kids screeched together.

"You about scared us to death, Christina!" Grant said. "And trust me, none of us can stand many more scares."

Christina hopped into the gazebo. "Why?" she asked eagerly. "What happened on your searches?"

The other kids began to talk at once, each telling their adventure nonstop and waving clues in her face.

"But they all sound just like the other clues," said Grant.

"But there are a gazillion of them!" added Thomas.

All the kids grew quiet, exhausted from recounting their experiences. Finally, McKenzie said, "What did you find, Christina?"

Christina shrugged. "I found Mr. Manse's office and a note that talked about a will but nothing that helps solve the mystery of the clues and what's going on around here to try to scare us off from opening a book shop."

"So we're at a dead end?" Grant asked.

"Afraid so," Christina said with a sigh.

"Hey, have any of you noticed anything?" said Thomas.

"What?" asked McKenzie, turning around. "I can't see a thing."

"That's what I mean," said Thomas. "It's pitch black dark...and your grandparents aren't back yet."

"Oh, yeah," said Grant.

"That's very strange," added Christina.

"We don't need any more strange," said McKenzie.

For a moment the kids were silent, listening to frogs burp and crickets chirp. Then Thomas said, "What we need is to finish our search."

"What are you talking about?" asked Christina. "We've covered every last inch of the house, top to bottom..."

Grant interrupted her. "And then some. I forgot to tell you I found a secret panel in a wall and a hidden staircase!"

The other kids gasped. "Where did they go?" they asked.

"Uh," began Grant, "I sort of chickened out. It was scary, you know! I was not gonna go down that spiral staircase all by myself."

In the darkness, Christina put out her arm to search for her brother's shoulder. She gave him a squeeze. "It's ok, Grant. We sure don't blame you. We would have chickened out too."

"Well, just because Grant didn't want to go down there alone doesn't mean that we can't all go down there together, right?" asked McKenzie.

"I think we should search the grounds," insisted Thomas. "There's that weird brick building. We have no idea what's in there. And the chapel. And..."

"I have an idea," said Christina. "McKenzie and I will go down the spiral staircase. You and Grant search the brick toolshed building. We'll do it fast and meet back here in ten or fifteen minutes, before Mimi and Papa show up. It may be our last chance to save the shop."

"Here's a flashlight," said Thomas, shoving one at Christina. "Do you girls have one?"

"Yes," said McKenzie, snapping hers on and almost blinding them all.

"Ok, then," said Christina. "Just be careful you guys. And don't forget our GERONIMO code word to call for help."

"I'm not too happy about this," Grant admitted.

"None of us are," Christina agreed. "But it's like the dentist—let's just get it over with."

"But I LIKE the dentist," Grant grumbled. "She gives me stickers and suckers...not *goosebumps!*"

No one answered. The girls had already headed off, and so had Thomas. "Hey!" squealed Grant. "Wait for me! Don't leave me here in the gory gazebo, please!"

When Grant heard Thomas giggle, he followed the sound into the darkness.

18
NOWHERE TO GO BUT UP...OR DOWN?

Christina did not turn on the flashlight until they reached the house. Once they went inside, she used it to get to the second floor and to try to find the room that had the secret panel in the wall.

When they thought they were in the right room, the girls began to *pat pat pat* the walls until suddenly, one flew open, whirling them into another room.

"Look!" said Christina, pointing the flashlight to the floor. "The wall moves, but there's a turntable in the floor—that's how we both just seemed to float into this room."

"Maybe this is how they moved dead bodies around the house?" McKenzie speculated.

"Let's don't think of that right now, please," begged Christina, but since it had been said, that's all they both envisioned.

Next they shoved on the walls trying to find the secret staircase. Just when they were about to give up, the wall opened and revealed the spiral staircase Grant had described. The girls stared downward, following the blade of light as it landed on each step. But they could not see past the turn.

"Ready?" asked Christina, stepping onto the first step.

"Not really," said McKenzie, "but I'm right behind you."

Cautiously, the girls inched down the steps.

In the backyard, the boys edged their way toward the brick house that Papa had guessed was for equipment or tools. The structure was small, but sturdy. A wave of the flashlight showed more recent patches of repair, which seemed surprising.

The building was almost covered in kudzu, all except the small door, which faced away from the house. On tiptoe, Grant and Thomas sneaked around to that side of the building.

"It smells funny," noted Grant.

"Maybe it was an old barbecue pit?" guessed Thomas, who swung the flashlight beam over the door where the boys saw a sign.

"Hey!" said Grant. "It says it's a CREMATORIUM. That sounds more like, uh, ice cream than barbecue to me."

"Whatever," muttered Thomas, trying the door handle. To the boys' surprise, the door opened easily.

Assuming that the building was indeed a storage shed, or something similar, they went right inside, following the narrow beam of light. They stood in the middle of the small room to look around.

"Smells like an oven in here," said Grant. *"Phew-wee!"*

"Look!" said Thomas. "There's a cot. And a table and chair. Think someone lives here?"

Grant chuckled. "No way! Not in this dirty, stinky place. That stuff must just be stored here. Move on inside."

As they boys made their way to the back wall and into what looked like a narrow hallway, they were surprised to find themselves slowly making their way *down down down* through a narrow tunnel.

After awhile, they came to a place where it leveled out.

About that time...the flashlight went out and they were plunged into total darkness!

Meanwhile, Christina and McKenzie continued to make their way down the spiral staircase and through a warren of narrow hallways.

"Where are we going?" asked McKenzie, frustrated. "I feel like we just keep backtracking."

"I know," said Christina. "I thought this looked like maybe where the hot water boiler would be, or the heating unit...hot water heater...maybe a washer and dryer. Surely they had to wash something now and then, even at a funeral home."

"*Especially* in a funeral home!" suggested McKenzie with a shiver.

"Well, we're not finding anything here, so let's try to make our way back to the staircase," said Christina, taking another turn.

McKenzie followed, but each time they turned, and were sure they'd run into the staircase, it was either a brick wall dead end, or another passage that looked just like the one they'd just been in.

"I don't like the way it smells down here," McKenzie complained.

"Well, I don't like..." Christina began, crankily, then hesitated, "uh, the way this flashlight is acting up." She shook the flashlight to try to get more light, but instead, with a blink, the light went out.

Both girls screamed and hugged one another.

19
GERONIMO!

Grant and Thomas were petrified. Christina and McKenzie were scared out of their wits. Neither pair knew exactly what to do. They had never been in such a sticky wicket situation before.

"Come on," Grant said finally, grasping Thomas by the forearm. "Let's just keep moving forward. This tunnel is bound to go somewhere." Thomas nodded in the darkness.

"Follow me," Christina insisted to McKenzie. "If we keep walking, I feel sure we will find the staircase." But she did not sound too certain about that.

"What choice do we actually have?" McKenzie said, as she held on to the back of Christina's tee shirt.

Slowly, all the children made their way forward, or they hoped that they had not gotten hopelessly turned around. It was darker than dark, darker than night, and scarier than any movie they'd ever watched.

Grant thought of Papa and wished he would come and rescue them.

Thomas thought of mice, rats, spiders, and such.

McKenzie thought of her mother and father and how they always warned her about getting into trouble—and here she was smack-dab in the middle of it!

Christina thought about Mimi and how distressed she would be if she returned to the Old Manse Funeral Home and could not find the children. What if she thought they'd hitched a ride home and left them behind? Christina decided not to think anymore, but just to walk...one...tentative...scary...step... at...a...time:

BUMP! BUMP! BUMP! BUMP!

Christina screamed!

McKenzie screamed!

The **acoustics** in the tunnel caused the screams to echo repeatedly against the walls.

Grant hollered at the top of his lungs!

Thomas yelled even louder.

Suddenly, all four children, unsure of what they had just bumped into, screamed the same word:

"GERONINO!"

"GERONIMO!"

"GERONIMO!"

"GERONOMO!"

They jumped up and down in place, brushing their arms, still bumping into...into...

"Grant? Is that you? Stop hollering!" cried Christina.

"Christina? McKenzie?" Grant said, amazed. Was he dreaming he wondered. "Where are you?"

"Right HERE!" McKenzie said, reaching out and touching Grant's arm, which just made him start screaming again.

"HUSH!!!!!" screamed Thomas. The children froze in place and got quiet. All you could hear was their heavy breathing.

"Christina," Grant said, at last, "why are you girls in our tunnel?"

"Why are you boys over in the house down the staircase?" Christina demanded. "Were you trying to scare us?"

"Ohhhh," said McKenzie. "You know what? I think our stairs must have led down beneath the ground!"

"You must be right!" said Thomas. "Our tunnel from the little building went down and down. We must have met in the middle."

"But in the middle of what?" asked Grant. "And didn't you girls have a flashlight?"

"Yes," said Christina, "but it's dead. Yours, too?"

"Afraid so," said Grant. "What do we do now?"

For a moment the kids were quiet. Then a voice cackled and said, "Well, you tried screaming 'GERONIMO' and that sure didn't help!" The voice cackled again.

Again, the children were quiet.

"*G-G-Grant?* Was that you making that weird laugh?" asked Christina.

"N-N-No," said Grant.

"Then who was it?" Christina asked, a tremble in her voice.

The cackly voice answered, "ME!"

The four kids screamed and began to run! In the turmoil in the tunnel, they were not sure which direction they were running or who they were running into. All they could hear was more screaming, more cackly laughter, and the *slap slap slap* of desperate footsteps as they tried to escape!

20
A DEAD END?

As it turned out, all four kids ended up running through the tunnel that led to the small building. One after another they reached the small room and bounded out the door into the yard.

As each child held their sides and leaned over toward the cool, damp grass to catch their breaths, heavy breathing was all they could hear.

One by one they stood up and peered at each other in the darkness.

"I'm taking roll!" Christina said. "Put your hand on my arm when I call your name!"

"Grant?" Grant touched her arm.

"McKenzie?" McKenzie grabbed her friend's hand tightly.

"Thomas?" Thomas grabbed onto Christina's forearm.

"Well, good," Christina said, with a sigh of relief. "At least we are all here safe and sound. Thank goodne—"

Suddenly, Christina felt a strange hand touch her arm.

"Yes, thank goodness!" said the crackly voice with a laugh.

The kids began to jump and scream again. Then suddenly, a gigantic light beamed on them.

"What's going on?" asked Papa. "What is all this yelling about? It sounds like a bunch of banshees back here!"

"Papa!" cried Christina. "Thank goodness! We are SO glad to see you!"

Mimi looked at the four big-eyed children. Uh, no...five pairs of big eyes stared back at her from the beam of light. "And who is this?" she asked in a shocked voice.

Papa turned the light on the fifth person and they all gasped. "Who are you?" he demanded.

"Wilbur," said the cackly voice. "I'm WILBUR!"

21
WILBUR

It took a long time to sort it all out.

First, Papa insisted that they all go in the house. He and Mimi were running late because they'd gone by the power company to get the electricity turned on.

And so, beneath a bare light bulb in the parlor, they sat on folding chairs and talked.

Wilbur was very old, not much bigger than a kid, and thrilled to be the center of attention. It was quickly clear that he was harmless, even trying to be friendly and play along with the kids in the tunnel. Christina figured he must be very lonesome. He'd obviously lived here in **seclusion** for many years.

"I live here," Wilbur explained. He pointed a bony thumb in the direction of the backyard.

"In the little brick building?" asked Papa gently.

Wilbur nodded.

"It's a crematorium," Grant said. "I read the sign on the building when we went inside, and boy, I could go for some ice cream about now...we missed dinner, you know."

"CREMATORIUM!" said Mimi. She looked like she might faint.

"Now, calm down," Papa said, patting her arm. "You know, back then a funeral home was likely to have a place to cremate bodies."

The four kids stared at Papa. They had lots of questions but it was clear that Papa was not interested in answering them at this particular time.

"But who ARE you, Wilbur?" Papa asked again, even more gently.

Suddenly, Christina snapped her fingers. "I know who he is," she said softly.

"How do you know?" Mimi asked, a confused and worried look on her face.

Christina explained. "I found Mr. Manse's office. Look!"

She held out the note she had picked up. "I think Mr. Manse wanted to leave everything to Wilbur—see, it says 'Wilb' here."

Wilbur hung his head. "My brother," he said sadly.

Mimi and Papa exchanged serious glances.

"Wilbur, have you lived here a long time?" Mimi asked. She put her hand gently on the man's bony forearm.

Wilbur nodded. "In the building. I grow veggies. I hide when people come...but no one comes...not till them." He pointed at the four kids and smiled. "I like them. They are fun!"

In spite of themselves, the four kids smiled back.

"You're fun, too, Wilbur," Grant said. "I guess you used to play around here when you were a kid?"

Wilbur surprised them all by hanging his head and weeping.

22
SHOP TALK

By the time the story was totally sorted out, with the help of Mr. Manse's diary, it became known that Wilbur was his younger brother, who had been left behind after Mr. Manse's death. There was no other family.

Wilbur was fine physically, for someone in his nineties, but his mind had always been that of a small child. He was harmless, but clearly resourceful to live here for so long on his own.

There were many decisions to be made, but Mimi was a very decisive person.

"Here's what we'll do," she explained. "We will clean up the, uh, crematorium, and Wilbur can live there as long as he likes. After all, it's the only home he's known for so many years. We will be sure he has health care and groceries, and—friendship."

"We'll get a lawyer," Papa added, and be sure Mr. Manse's will is re-executed per the note Christina found, so that Wilbur inherits as he should have long ago."

"But won't that mean he owns this old house?" Christina couldn't help but ask.

Mimi nodded and Christina spotted the disappointment in her grandmother's eyes. "And he can do whatever he wants to with the place," Mimi said. "It belongs to him." She gave Wilbur a big smile, and a hug.

But it turned out that what Wilbur wanted to do was what he had overheard, eavesdropping on them all. Through his new social worker he had made it clear he wanted Mimi to own the house and land. He just wanted to stay in his little building as he always had. And so the lawyers drew up the papers to make all that legal and proper.

Papa and Uncle Michael helped put the building in good repair and Mimi redecorated

Wilbur's room. Dad made a new sign that said WILBUR'S PLACE and put it up where the old sign had been. Wilbur had beamed.

The guys had redone the yard, painted the chapel, and planted purple wisteria, and other old-timey plants. They also cleaned the tombstones till they gleamed, painted the house, inside and out, and hung ferns on the porch, which now held white, wicker rockers with comfy, fat cushions.

Once the house was spic-and-span, Mimi began work on the shop, with the help of all the kids of course. It went something like this:

• Christina decorated the PARLOR to be a lovely reception room and check-out area.

• Aunt Cassidy and Ella turned the embalming room into the Tombstone Tea Room. The new kitchen was bright and white and cheerful. The back porch held ice-cream-parlor-style tables and chairs which were also scattered among the tombstones, which, it turned out, were just for show—not a real cemetery—so folks could see what kind of lovely tombstones were available for sale.

• Grant and Thomas cleaned out the basement, and once it was fixed up, it became a place kids could come for Story Hour and to do crafts. It was the most popular place in town and on any rainy Saturday, you could find Mimi reading aloud to scads of delighted kids.

• Uncle Michael set up the Accounting Office in Mr. Manse's old office and Dad set up the shop's computer system. The big, old, roll-top desk came in handy with all its cubbyholes. When Papa worked in there, he stuck special notes up on the antlers of some of the animals on the wall, so he'd be sure to remember the shop tasks Mimi gave him. Mr. Manse's diary sits there on a **pedestal** to this day.

• Mom and Christina set up all the other downstairs rooms with Mimi's many, many books. When they ran out of room, they headed up to the second floor. Fiction, nonfiction, state books, mysteries—there was something for every age and interest. Papa insisted they make a special room for cowboy books and didn't complain when that turned into an A-Z section of all kind of interesting subjects from Alligators to Zombies.

• In the attic, Christina and Mom decided to clean it all up, then leave it empty. When Mimi asked, "WHY?!" Christina and Mom just laughed and said, "Because we are sure you will write MORE books, Mimi!" Mimi had nodded and asked them to set up a writing desk by the front window in the turret so she could look out and see customers come and go as she worked.

It took a lot of work to get everything just right. Books had to be ordered and shelved, all had to be priced, and signs had to be made.

"There's only one problem, Mimi," Grant said. "We can't get a sign made until you decide what to call your shop."

Mimi thought and thought and thought. "Well," she said, "I guess I always thought it would be called The Book Shop."

"Boring!" Grant muttered under his breath.

"Not Mimi-ish at all!" Christina agreed.

Mimi thought some more. "Well, you kids sure thought this place was full of ghosts for awhile, didn't you?"

The kids all nodded.

"We sure did, and if we had never met Wilbur, we would still think this place is haunted!" said Grant.

Mimi folded her arms and smiled.

"Oh, I get it!" cried Grant. "You're going to name this place..." He held out his arms to the other kids to help him out. One by one, they each nodded in understanding and yelled in unison:

"MIMI'S HAUNTED BOOK SHOP!"

23

MIMI'S HAUNTED BOOK SHOP

And so the sign was made and hung. Mimi proudly held a Grand Opening and ribbon-cutting ceremony. All Mimi's fans came from near and far. They shopped for books, rocked in the rockers, and enjoyed homemade lemonade and book-shaped brownies in the tearoom and garden.

It was great fun! The newspapers came and did stories on the funeral parlor turned book shop, and about Mimi and Wilbur and the history of the Old Manse Place.

Grant complained. "They should tell the cool part—about all our wild and crazy adventures here."

"Don't worry," said Christina, throwing her arm around her brother's shoulder. "You know Mimi will put it all in a book one day!"

After the ribbon-cutting out front, Papa gathered everyone in the backyard. He and Wilbur tugged on an enormous white work cloth that had covered the gazebo for weeks.

When the cloth fell to the ground, Mimi clapped her hands together in glee. "Papa!" she exclaimed, giving him such a big, fat kiss it knocked his cowboy hat off—again.

Papa had painted the gazebo snow white, added hanging baskets of colorful flowers around all the sides, hung a crystal chandelier in the center, and installed a dance floor! He and Mimi loved to dance and when Wilbur started the music, that's just what they did!

The kids all laughed, none louder than Wilbur, who cackled loudly with joy.

AND LATER...

• Uncle Michael built a fishpond and filled it with "red herrings."

•A black cat and a white cat took up residence at the shop. Mimi named them Dewey and Decimal.

•Papa brought a big, old, gray-and-white English Sheepdog ("for security!") and to keep Wilbur company. Mimi named him Bookie and he loved greeting customers with a wag of his bobbed tail and a lick from his fat pink tongue!

• Avery, Ella, and Evan turned the Secret Staircase into a special reading room just for little kids.

• Mimi filled up the attic with new books!

Lastly, one day Mimi said, "You know, not all my readers from far away can come to my book shop. What we really need is a website, Grant...where is that website you were going to make?"

Please visit mimishauntedbookshop.com.

And remember, "What you believe—you can achieve!"

HAPPY READING!

Now...go to
www.carolemarshmysteries.com
and...

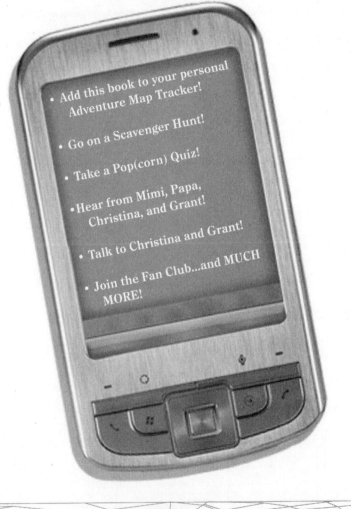

- Add this book to your personal Adventure Map Tracker!

- Go on a Scavenger Hunt!

- Take a Pop(corn) Quiz!

- Hear from Mimi, Papa, Christina, and Grant!

- Talk to Christina and Grant!

- Join the Fan Club...and MUCH MORE!

GLOSSARY

ascertain: to determine or figure out

banshee: a wailing spirit

contemporary: modern

dingy: faded, dirty

envision: imagine

faux: (pronounced FOE); fake

ferret: search or seek; also a kind of polecat

liquidate: to sell property to get the cash

listless: tired; out of energy

loll: to sprawl around lazily

red herrings: in a mystery, characters the author uses to mislead the reader

sashay: exaggerated walk

spic-and-span: fresh and clean

SAT GLOSSARY

acoustics: the way sounds can be heard in a particular room or space; *"A symphony hall needs good acoustics."*

candid: honest, forthcoming, true feelings; *"She was candid with me about her hurt feelings."*

grandiose: big, imposing, meant to impress; *"The grandiose palace got everyone's attention."*

pedestal: a post or column with a top; often used to showcase a piece of art; also, to *"put someone on a pedestal"* out of admiration... sometimes, they fall off their pedestal!

seclusion: to live alone, often by choice, avoiding other people; *"He lived in seclusion because he was old, tired, and had grown very unsociable."*

AND ALSO...

Dewey Decimal is ...the letter and numbering system in which library books are generally arranged!

Geronimo was...a famous Apache Indian chief and warrior.

Enjoy this exciting excerpt from:

THE MYSTERY AT
Area 51

1
A LITTLE TURBULENCE!

Christina unlocked her flower-patterned diary and set it in her lap. She ran her fingers over the embossed outer cover.

The last time Christina wrote in it was three years ago. She kept it in her glittery "keepsake shoebox" in the back of her closet—that is, until this trip.

"You've brought your diary, Christina," Mimi said over the roar of the airplane's engine. Mimi wore her blonde hair short. Her gem-studded glasses hung from her neck by a simple chain. She was "co-piloting" the *Mystery Girl* with her pilot husband, Papa. To her, he was a cowboy through and through. His tall rugged frame wouldn't be complete without a Stetson hat, jeans, and cowboy boots.

Christina and her younger brother, Grant, often traveled with their globe-trotting grandparents, Mimi and Papa, on vacation, while Mimi, a children's mystery writer, collected research for her books.

On this particular trip, Mimi planned to do research on Nevada mining ghost towns.

Their first stop—the Alamo, Nevada, landing strip of Papa's good friend, Mr. Colton Hayes. He went by "Buck," though, plain and simple. Buck and his wife, Nina, raised cattle on their 1,200-acre ranch.

"Yes, Mimi," Christina answered. "I brought this diary the first time we stayed at Buck's ranch three years ago."

"I remember that," Mimi said, smiling. "I recall that you got pretty good at drawing on that trip."

"Thanks, Mimi. I wish I could say the same about my spelling back then," Christina admitted. She tucked her long, brown hair behind her ears and looked over at Grant. He was fast asleep with his mouth gaping open. She turned to the first page of her diary. It read,

Propertey of Christina! Privite!

Christina fought the urge to correct her childish spelling. She continued to leaf through her diary and came to a page illustrated with desert flowers, their names obviously copied from an encyclopedia:

'Hedgehog cactus'—purple petals. *'Claret Cup cactus'*—red petals. *'Coulter's Lupine'*—purple and yellow.

Christina remembered the big lesson she learned three years ago: *Take only photographs. Leave only footprints.* She didn't have a camera, so she did the next best thing: she drew pictures—and lots of them!

Just then, a photo fell out of the diary and fluttered to the floor.

Christina hesitated before unbuckling her seatbelt, and then thought better of it. She flipped off her shoes, and using her toes, scooped up the photo.

Suddenly, the plane banked hard to the right. Her diary slid off her lap and disappeared under the seat in front of her.

Christina glanced back to check on her brother. The good news was that Grant was still buckled in. The bad news was he was upside down in his seat!

Is that even possible? she wondered.

Suddenly, Grant lifted his head, eyes still glued shut. "I want to put the spaceship together by myself!" he mumbled. Then, he plopped his head back down.

From the rumbling cockpit, Papa called out over his shoulder, "Minor turbulence! Nothing to worry about! Are you youngin's OK?"

"I'm fine!" Christina answered. "Grant is still sound asleep!"

Mimi looked over her shoulder and did a double-take. "He's really asleep like that?" she asked.

"Yep! He manages to be goofy even when he's asleep!" Christina joked. "Mimi, should we wake him up now?"

"Ten more minutes, OK?" Mimi said. "Otherwise, we'll have a little grouch on our hands."

Mimi leaned closer to Papa. Over the roar of the engine, Christina caught only a handful of words exchanged—near miss... strange object...mid-air...fifty-one...

Christina reached down to retrieve the photo from between her feet. She turned it over. In the picture, a younger Grant was standing in a giant tire swing hanging from an old oak tree. His bright blue eyes peered over the top of the tire. His signature curly-blonde hair framed a smiling face.

Megan and Drew, brother and sister, sat playing cards on a picnic blanket. They were about the same ages as Christina and Grant. Christina was standing under the tree, pointing at something in the sky. She looked puzzled.

Seeing herself in the old photo, Christina wondered, *What was I looking at in that blue November sky?*

Just then, Grant woke up from his dream with such a start that Christina jumped in her seat!

Grant's curly hair was matted down on one side. Christina couldn't help but laugh. "Grant, your hair!" she said and giggled.

Grant flipped right side up. He was annoyed at being laughed at, but was even more bothered that they let him sleep upside down.

"At least you didn't fall on your head, Grant," Christina teased. "You might have broken the floor!"

"Ha ha, you are such a genius!" Grant said.

"The correct term is child prodigy, little brother!" Christina said and laughed.

Christina looked out at the Mojave Desert through the plane's small window. Spiky cactus plants and Joshua trees dotted the landscape. There, on the **outskirts** of the desert, sprung an oasis of lush, green countryside.

"Mimi, look down!" Christina said. She popped the earphones out of her ears and stuffed her music player in her backpack.

"We must be close!" Mimi exclaimed.

"Finally!" Grant said.

"Well, crew, it looks like we're cleared for landing," Papa announced.

Christina's heart skipped a beat. She was eager to stand on solid ground. But she was nervous.

What if my old friends don't remember me? she thought.

"Look, I see Buck waving by the barn," Grant yelled. "Papa, I think he wants you to circle around," he warned.

"Grant's right, Papa! Look, there's a bull on the landing strip!" shouted Christina. "Buck needs to get him out of there!"

2
A CRIME AGAINST COWS

The *Mystery Girl* landed safely. Mimi hopped out onto the runway. Her red sneakers contrasted sharply with the black asphalt. The Nevada sun was beginning to set in the west.

Grant threw himself onto the ground. "Solid ground! You are my best friend in the whole wide world!" he cried.

"Grant! Here come Buck and Nina," Christina warned. She couldn't help but smile at her little brother's antics. He hopped up, ready to greet them.

A tall man with gray sideburns and sporting a white cowboy hat and leather boots approached the *Mystery Girl*. It was Buck, Papa's friend.

"Welcome to the Flyin' "R," folks! It's great to see ya'll again!" he roared.

Buck gave Papa a big bear hug. "Hello, good friend!" he said. "Sorry about that little inconvenience on the runway. Bulls and airplanes don't mix real well!"

His wife, Nina, a small, gray-haired woman, smiled warmly. Her hair was pulled back in a tidy bun. She wore a blue checkered apron over a t-shirt and jeans. Dust covered her tan cowboy boots.

"Buck and Nina, you remember Grant and Christina," Mimi said.

"My, you two have certainly grown!" Buck said. "The grandchildren are out getting supplies to make S'mores for the bonfire tonight."

"Megan and Drew begged their parents to let them come this week because they knew you two would be here!" Nina said.

Christina could finally exhale. *This vacation just might be something to write home about after all!*

Mimi and Nina walked ahead, arm-in-arm, chatting like no time had passed between visits.

Buck and Papa laughed heartily and slapped each other on the back as they unloaded the luggage from the plane.

At the ranch house, Mimi and the kids enjoyed tart homemade lemonade. Chunky ice cubes clinked in the tall glasses.

In the family room, a roaring fire burned brightly in a massive stone fireplace. Through a giant window bare of curtains, a pristine lake sparkled in the evening light. The setting sun cast brilliant hues of oranges and reds on the lake and the mountainous horizon beyond it.

"You all might want to freshen up a bit. We're having barbecue," Nina announced.

"Barbecue!" Grant shouted. He pumped his fist in the air. "I'm starving!"

"Oh, I hear Papa," Mimi said. "I'll be back in a minute."

The kids nodded. Nina led the way to their room. Her slippers slapped the floor as she walked. "Grant, quick, your shoes," Christina whispered, and pointed to Nina's retreating slippers. She gathered up their dusty sneakers.

Nina disappeared around a corner. Grant skated after her in his socks.

Christina heard Mimi and Papa talking in an adjacent room. "Mimi, what should I do with our shoes? Mimi?" She peeked in the room where she thought the voices were coming from but no one was there.

A long dining room table with enough chairs to seat an army sat in the middle of a massive dining room. A newspaper clipping lay on the middle of the table. Christina read it and gasped. She hurried from the room and ran smack into Grant!

Rubbing his head, Grant said, "Christina, where did you go?"

"Grant, you'll never believe what I just saw!" she exclaimed.

Grant's wide-eyed expression urged Christina to continue. "A newspaper article about cow abductions!"

"I've heard of cow patties, cowhide, and cows jumping over the moon, but I've never heard of cow and duck shins!" Grant said.

"Cow abductions, meaning cows being taken!" Christina exclaimed.

"Taken?" he asked. "Taken by who?"

"Not who! What!" she cried. "The newspaper article said it was aliens!" she exclaimed.